Molly Bang

TEN, NINE, EIGHT

Greenwillow Books, New York

Library of Congress Cataloging in Publication Data

Bang, Molly. Ten, nine, eight.
"Greenwillow Books."
Summary: Numbers from ten to one are
part of this lullaby which observes the room
of a little girl going to bed.
[1. Lullabies. 2. Counting.] I. Title.
II. Title: 10, 9, 8.
PZ8.3.B22Te [E] 81-20106
ISBN 0-688-00906-9
ISBN 0-688-00907-7 (lib. bdg.)
ISBN 0-688-10480-0 (pbk.)
ISBN 0-688-15468-9 (Spanish pbk.—*Diez, Nueve, Ocho*)

First Edition 35 34 33 32 31

FOR DEBORAH,
PRESHIEL, SYLVIA, VIKI
AND THEIR CHILDREN
AND FOR
DICK AND MONIKA,
WITH THANKS
AND
LOVE

10 small toes all washed and warm

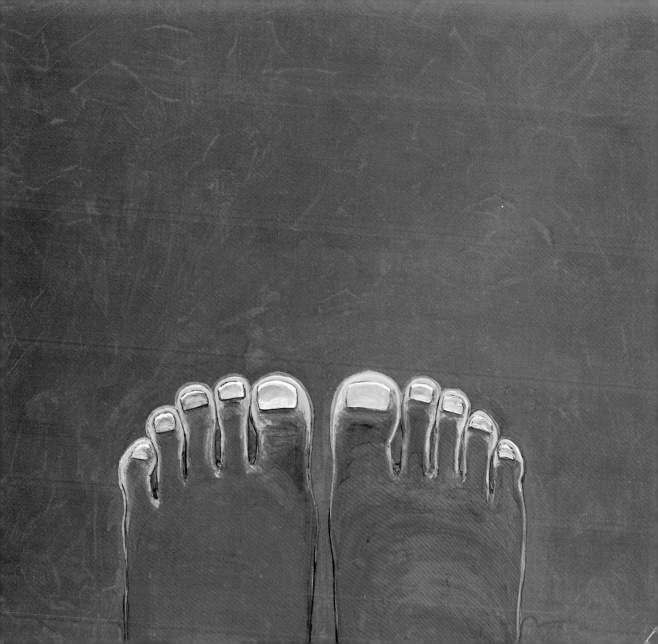

9 soft friends
in a quiet room

8 square windowpanes with falling snow

7 empty shoes in a short straight row

6 pale seashells
hanging down

5 round buttons on a yellow gown

4 sleepy eyes which open and close

3 loving kisses on cheeks and nose

2 strong arms around a fuzzy bear's head

1 big girl all ready for bed